UNICORNS
OF THE
SECRET STABLE

Starberry
Magic

JOLLY
FiSH
PRESS

Mendota Heights, Minnesota

By Whitney Sanderson
Illustrated by Jomike Tejido

Book design by Sarah Taplin
Illustrations by Jomike Tejido
Illustrations on pages 30, 39, 46, 57 by North Star Editions

Published in the United States by Jolly Fish Press, an imprint of North Star Editions, Inc.

First Edition
First Printing, 2020

This is a work of fiction. Names, characters, places, and incidents are either the product of the author's imagination or are used fictitiously, and any resemblance to actual persons living or dead, business establishments, events, or locales is entirely coincidental.

Library of Congress Cataloging-in-Publication Data (pending)
978-1-63163-505-2 (paperback)
978-1-63163-504-5 (hardcover)

Jolly Fish Press
North Star Editions, Inc.
2297 Waters Drive
Mendota Heights, MN 55120
www.jollyfishpress.com

Printed in the United States of America

TABLE OF CONTENTS

Unicorn Guardians

A long time ago, unicorns and people lived together. When people started hunting the unicorns, two girls decided to help. They used unicorn magic to create a powerful spell. It closed off the Enchanted Realm from the rest of the world. Only the girls' keys could open the Magic Gate.

When the girls grew up, they gave the keys to their daughters. Since then, two young girls have always been the Unicorn Guardians.

CHAPTER 1

Meadowsweet's Discovery

Ruby ducked low on Meadowsweet's neck. A bright red ember whizzed over her head. It landed on the ground with a hiss. Gray smoke rose from a volcano in the distance.

Pools of lava bubbled on the ground. Meadowsweet stepped carefully around them.

It was Ruby's first time exploring the Fire Mountains. Dragons lived here.

Sometimes they attacked unicorns.

But Ruby's friend Cole was the Dragon

Guardian now. He had told the dragons

to leave the unicorns alone.

Meadowsweet sniffed the air. She made a sharp turn to the left. They went around a large boulder. Ruby spotted a patch of thorny bushes. Berries grew on their branches. Ruby had never seen anything like the berries before.

The berries were pearly white. They were shaped like tiny stars. And they were glowing.

Ruby slid down from Meadowsweet's back. She picked one of the shining starberries and sniffed it. Was it safe to eat?

Meadowsweet stretched out her neck. She gobbled up the berry and nodded.

Starberry Magic

If unicorns could eat the berries, people could eat them safely too. Ruby picked another berry. She popped it into her mouth.

It tasted a little like her favorite fruit, strawberries. But it also tasted like her favorite dessert, chocolate cookies. And it fizzed like her favorite drink, ginger ale.

Ruby filled her pockets with berries.

Starberry Magic

She hardly noticed the sharp thorns scratching her hands. She couldn't wait to share the berries with her sister, Iris.

Iris was a Unicorn Guardian, like Ruby. But Iris was afraid to explore the Fire Mountains.

Ruby rode Meadowsweet back out of the Fire Mountains. They returned to the sunny field where the unicorns lived.

Ruby dismounted from Meadowsweet's back. She let Meadowsweet gallop off to join the herd.

Ruby walked to the Magic Gate at the end of the meadow. She went through it and locked the gate with her key. The unicorns disappeared behind her.

Now the meadow looked like an empty pasture. Next to the pasture was an old red barn with a sign that said Magic Moon Stable.

Across the yard was the farmhouse where Ruby's family lived. Her mom was waiting for her inside.

"There you are," she said to Ruby. "I worried you forgot."

"Forgot what?" Ruby asked. "Oh! The baking contest!"

Her mom and her Aunt May owned a bakery called the Cupcake Castle.

It was hosting a baking contest for kids.

The first round was today. The top four

bakers would go on to the final round

next weekend. The winner would be the

Junior Baking Champion.

Ruby followed her mom out to the car. She was still thinking about the starberries. She snuck another one out of her pocket and ate it. Nothing had ever tasted so good.

She could hardly even remember what she had been planning to bake for the contest.

CHAPTER 2

Triple Chocolate Disaster

Eight junior bakers were working in the Cupcake Castle's large kitchen. The judge of the contest was Chef Pierre. He owned a popular restaurant in Summerville.

He would decide which bakers went on to the final round.

The contest winner would get an apron that said Junior Baking Champion. And the winning recipe would be printed in the newspaper.

Ruby walked up to her work station. It was already set up with mixing bowls, measuring cups, and ingredients.

Step number one was to read her recipe. A copy of the recipe she had chosen leaned against a bag of sugar. But she had only learned to read this year. She was still a little slow at it. She didn't have time to read the whole recipe. And she had baked her triple chocolate cookies before.

Ruby grabbed the bag of sugar and a

measuring cup. She started pouring and mixing. When she had finished, she tasted the dough.

Ugh, it was terrible!

Ruby looked closer at the bag of sugar in front of her. It said Salt. The bigger bag next to it was sugar. She'd been in such a hurry she had mixed up her ingredients.

Ruby felt tears welling up. She had practiced so hard for this contest. Now she would never make it to the final round.

She reached into her pocket for a tissue. She didn't want Chef Pierre and the other bakers to know she was crying over cookies.

Ruby's fingers brushed the starberries in her pocket. She scooped them up and held them in her hand. Could their sweetness make up for the extra salt? It was worth a try.

Ruby dropped the starberries into her mixing bowl and stirred. Soon they disappeared into the thick brown dough.

When the time was up, the bakers put their pies, cakes, and cookies on serving trays. Chef Pierre tasted them. He made comments to each baker.

Some of the kids had done well. Others had made mistakes. But no one else had used two cups of salt.

Chef Pierre tried Ruby's cookies last. She hadn't had time to taste them.

She waited for Chef Pierre to say they were awful.

But he didn't.

"Delicious," he said. "Ruby, you are the winner of this round. You will bake in the final round next weekend."

CHAPTER 3

Starberry Shortcake

Iris gave Ruby a big hug. But Ruby could hardly believe she had won. She had been sure the extra salt had ruined the cookies. She picked one up and took a bite.

It was the most delicious cookie she had ever eaten. How was that possible?

Ruby got a sinking feeling in her stomach. Many of the plants in the Enchanted Realm were magical. What if starberries made *everything* taste good, even salty cookies?

Ruby's mom and aunt came over to congratulate her on winning the round.

When Ruby and her family got home, Iris

gave Ruby a new wooden mixing spoon.

"I knew you could do it!" Iris said.

Ruby wanted to tell Iris about the starberries. But she did not want Iris to know she had messed up her cookies. Anyway, Ruby did not know for sure whether the starberries were magic.

"I'll make dessert tonight," Ruby said. "But I'm going to go play outside first."

Ruby went to the Enchanted Realm.

She found Meadowsweet in the herd of unicorns.

Ruby went over to her. "I need to find the starberries again," she said. "Can you help me?"

Meadowsweet let Ruby climb onto her back. They cantered off toward the Fire Mountains.

Ruby could not remember exactly where the berries were. The dry hills and valleys all looked the same to her. Everything was dusty and scorched.

But Meadowsweet had a good sense of smell. She lifted her head and sniffed the air. She wound her way among the sharp rocks until they found the starberry bushes.

Ruby picked a handful of the berries for Meadowsweet to eat. Then she filled her own pockets again.

As soon as Ruby got home, she started baking. The recipe was for strawberry shortcake. This time she messed up her baking on purpose.

She added licorice instead of vanilla to the batter. She used sour cream instead of whipped cream for the cake's topping. She covered the strawberries with lemon juice instead of sugar syrup. Last of all,

she mixed in the starberries.

Ruby's mom, Aunt May, and Iris were waiting in the dining room. Ruby served up heaping plates of shortcake.

Iris took a big forkful. Ruby hoped she would spit it out.

"Awesome!" Iris said with her mouth full.

"I think this is your best recipe yet," Aunt May said. She scraped her plate to get every drop of berry sauce.

Ruby sighed. She had been right. The starberries were the only reason she was still in the contest.

She could not use them in the final round of the contest. That would be cheating. But without them, how could she bake anything good enough to win?

The next day, Ruby went back to the Enchanted Realm. She sat in the meadow and watched the unicorns.

The stallions Tempest and Starfire were play fighting. The mare Heartsong was napping in the long grass with her twin foals. Ruby smiled at the sight.

Meadowsweet was grazing nearby. Her rainbow mane blew back in the breeze. Ruby could see the flower-shaped marking on her forehead. Each unicorn had its own special symbol.

Ruby often wished she could bring other people to the Enchanted Realm. It was hard to keep such a special place a secret. If only there was some way to share the magic.

"Maybe there is . . ." Ruby said out loud.

Meadowsweet lifted her head. She walked over to Ruby. She nudged Ruby's shoulder with her soft nose.

Ruby took a folded napkin out of her pocket. Inside was a piece of starberry shortcake. She fed it to Meadowsweet.

"Sorry, we can't go for a ride today," she said. "I have a new recipe to test!"

CHAPTER 4

A Magical Bake

Ruby walked into the kitchen of the Cupcake Castle. Chef Pierre was there. The bakers' families were there. Even a reporter from the newspaper was there.

Ruby greeted the other kids who had made it to the final round.

Oliver was ten. He made fancy things like peach foam and candied violets. Jade was nine. She had her own baking blog. Anna was eight. Last week, Chef Pierre had called her cinnamon buns "scrumptious."

Ruby was six. She had only been baking for a few months. But worrying wouldn't help her now. She had to bake.

So, she mixed. She stirred. She poured. She double-checked to make sure she was using sugar, not salt.

Chef Pierre helped her put her tray into the hot oven. Then, Ruby waited for twelve minutes. They felt like the longest minutes ever.

Finally, her cupcakes were done. It was time to decorate.

"Bakers, you have five minutes!" Chef Pierre said.

Ruby still had a few starberries left. If she used them now, she was sure to win. But then she would never know if she was a good baker.

Ruby picked up her frosting bag. She started piping as fast as she could.

"Bakers, your time is up!" Chef Pierre said.

Starberry Magic

Ruby, Oliver, Jade, and Anna set down their plates on a long table.

Jade had baked French sandwich cookies called macarons. Anna's pecan pie looked as scrumptious as last week's cinnamon buns. Oliver had used extra gelatin to make butterscotch pudding into tiny, round pearls. Ruby thought they looked like fish eggs.

Chef Pierre tasted each recipe. This time, he didn't say anything. Ruby could not tell what he was thinking.

She held her breath as he ate one of her cupcakes. The top was covered with rainbow frosting. It looked like Meadowsweet's mane. Ruby had made ears out of fondant, a kind of thick icing.

In the center of each cupcake was a unicorn horn. The horns were the pointy ends of ice cream cones. Below the horns, Ruby had made symbols out of fondant. Some cupcakes had flowers. Others had stars or clouds. Just like the unicorns in the Enchanted Realm.

Chef Pierre shook the bakers' hands.

He went and sat at a table in the corner.

He scribbled notes in a notebook.

When he came back over, he was holding a folded apron.

"This was a hard decision," he said. "But one baker showed the most creativity and skill today. The Junior Baking Champion is . . ."

He paused for what seemed like a century.

"Ruby!"

Chef Pierre lifted the apron over Ruby's head. She could hardly believe it. Everyone clapped and cheered for her.

"What's your secret, Ruby?" Chef Pierre asked.

"I wanted to bake something that would make people smile," Ruby said.

She remembered the starberries in her pocket. Later, she would feed them to the unicorns. She didn't need them to make something magical.

THINK ABOUT IT

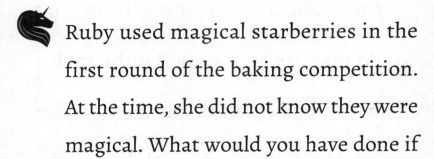 Ruby used magical starberries in the first round of the baking competition. At the time, she did not know they were magical. What would you have done if you were in the same situation?

Tell a friend about a time you were in a competition. It could be in school, in sports, or at home.

Do you like to bake? If so, what kinds of things do you like to bake?

ABOUT THE AUTHOR

Whitney Sanderson grew up riding horses as a member of a 4-H club and competing in local jumping and dressage shows. She has written several books in the Horse Diaries chapter book series. She is also the author of *Horse Rescue: Treasure*, based on her time volunteering at an equine rescue farm. She lives in Massachusetts.

ABOUT THE ILLUSTRATOR

Jomike Tejido is an author and illustrator of the picture book *There Was an Old Woman Who Lived in a Book*. He also illustrated the Pet Charms and My Magical Friends leveled reader series. He has fond memories of horseback riding as a kid and has always loved drawing magical creatures. Jomike lives in Manila with his wife, two daughters, and a chow chow named Oso.

RETURN TO MAGIC MOON STABLE

Book 1

Book 2

Book 3

Book 4

Book 5

Book 6

Book 7

Book 8

AVAILABLE NOW